LITTLE LOST
DRAGON

Dedicated to Joan Anderson,
with thanks to Caroline Roberts for her help.

A TEMPLAR BOOK

This softback edition published in the UK in 2009 by Templar Publishing,
an imprint of The Templar Company Limited,
The Granary, North Street, Dorking, Surrey, RH4 1DN, UK
www.templarco.co.uk

First published in 1992 by Hutchinson Children's Books
an imprint of the Random Century Group Ltd

ISBN 978-1-84011-750-9

Printed in China

LITTLE LOST
DRAGON

WAYNE ANDERSON

templar publishing

One morning, an egg dropped from the sky.

It fell down, down, into the deep, dark ocean and landed on the bottom. The water rocked it, and the quiet voices of the fish comforted it. Soon, a tiny crack appeared in the egg, which spread until the shell broke in two…

The baby creature looked at the watery world and called out for his mother and father. But the only reply was the welcoming murmur of the fish.

"Where is my family?" asked the creature. "And what am I?"

"We're not sure," the fish said. "Perhaps you're a fish – after all, you have scales and fins, like us."

The fish felt sorry for the baby creature, so they built him a house of shells and fed him meals of seaweed.

Soon the creature grew and grew until the fins on his back became tiny wings and the shell house was too small for him.

"I am not a fish," he said, looking at his wings. "I need to go and find my family who love me and my home where I belong."

So the creature swam to the shore where the bright sun warmed him. "Perhaps this is my home," the creature said. He waited and waited, but his family did not come.

Just then there was a loud buzzing sound as a dragonfly flew by.
"Where is my family?" asked the creature. "And what am I?"
"You have wings," said the dragonfly. "Perhaps you are an insect,
like me. Can you fly?"

The creature flapped and jumped, but he could not fly.
"Your wings are too new," said the dragonfly.
"You need to practise."

So the creature practised and practised. Finally,
he took off with a great whoosh!

"I am not a dragonfly," the creature thought, "because no insect has ever flown this high."

Suddenly, a flock of birds flew by. They squawked with surprise to see such a strange animal flying in the sky.

"What am I?" asked the creature.

"Perhaps you are a bird," they sang. "Fly with us to the jungle where the sun is always warm."

In the jungle, when the sun rose, the birds began to sing. The creature joined in, but his breath began to smoke and his voice was so loud that it shook the earth. The animals hid in fright.

"He's not a bird," they said. "His voice is like smoking thunder and he has scaly green skin. Go away, monster!" they cried, running into the long grass to hide.

"I'm not a bird," the creature whispered sadly to himself.

"What did you say?" asked a silky voice. Through the grass slithered a silvery snake.

"Are you part of my family?" the creature asked.

"I might be," said the snake. "I have scaly skin like yours. Can you wind yourself around and around, like me?"

The young creature tried, but he tied himself in knots that took all day to untangle.

"You're not a snake," said the python. "You must travel on if you want to find your family."

"I am not a fish, or an insect, or a bird, or a snake," the creature whispered, as he crossed the swampy marshland.

"No, my sweet – you are a crocodile," came a raspy voice, "and I am your mother. We both have scaly green skin and pointed claws and your teeth are sharp, just like mine. Come closer and I'll show you."

The crocodile opened its cavernous mouth and the creature suddenly knew what she had in mind.

"No, I am not a crocodile!" he cried, swiftly spreading his wings and flying high up into the sky.

The creature flew for many days, until he reached a grey, icy land.
    "MOTHER! FATHER! Where are you?" screeched the creature,
but there was no answer.
    Eventually he grew tired, and seeing a thin line of smoke trailing up
into the sky, the creature remembered the smoke he had made.
Flying closer, he saw a shape as large as himself, with big yellow eyes.

He glided down and looked into one of
the yellow eyes. Inside was a boy.
  "You are not like me," said the creature,
quietly – he didn't want to frighten him.
"But perhaps you can tell me what I am
and where my family is?"
  The boy looked up at the face at the
window. "You are a magical creature –
I'm reading about you in my book."
  And he held the book up so that the
creature could look at the picture.
  "My own kind!" the creature cried.
"Can you tell me how to find them?"

"We can use the map in my book as a guide," said the boy, putting on his scarf and coat and climbing up onto the creature's back. "We must go north, to the edge of the Earth, where magic is at its strongest."

As they flew through the night, it grew colder and colder, and the creature's wings grew heavier and heavier, until finally he had to stop and rest.

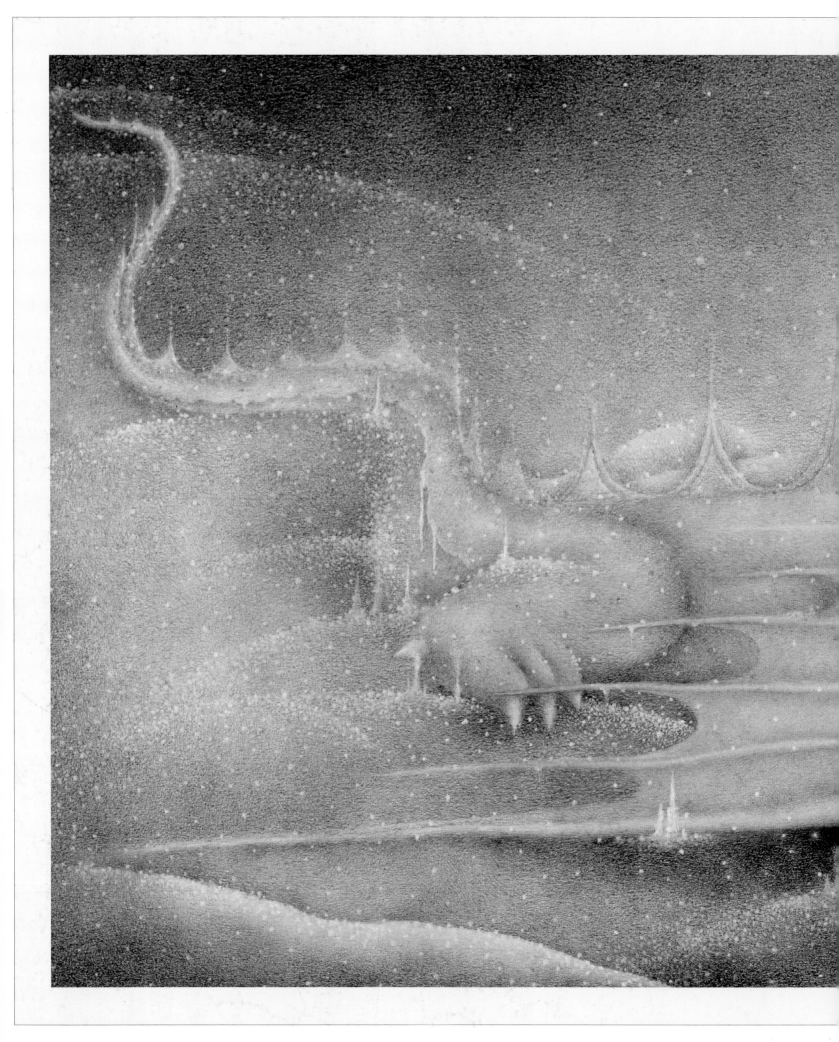

In the morning the two friends woke to find themselves frozen to the ground.

"Oh!" cried the creature. "We are trapped here. Now we will die and I will never find my family."

"Wait," said the boy. "It says in my book that you can make fire."

The creature took a deep breath and blew. Huge flames of red and orange shot from his mouth, lighting up the sky. The fire warmed the icy cage that trapped them, melting it into the snow.

U p they flew again, across the frozen lands to the edge of the world.

"There's your home," said the boy, pointing to a high mountain. Suddenly a group of magnificent winged creatures appeared – all with green, scaly skin and sharp, pointed teeth. The biggest of them flew up and cried, "My son!"

The young creature knew that voice – it was from the time before his search began, from before he had hatched. At last he knew he had found his home. The creature lowered the boy onto the snow, then flew to his mother. She wrapped him in her great wings and held him close.

"Now you are where you belong," she said, "and your name is…"

"...DRAGON."